Memories in the Land of Stardust

by

Sharon De Pontes

Creative Editor Jason Kolodzyk

DORRANCE
PUBLISHING CO
EST. 1920
PITTSBURGH, PENNSYLVANIA 15238

The contents of this work, including, but not limited to, the accuracy of events, people, and places depicted; opinions expressed; permission to use previously published materials included; and any advice given or actions advocated are solely the responsibility of the author, who assumes all liability for said work and indemnifies the publisher against any claims stemming from publication of the work.

Dorrance Publishing Co
585 Alpha Drive
Suite 103
Pittsburgh, PA 15238
Visit our website at *www.dorrancebookstore.com*

ISBN: 978-1-4809-3088-9
eISBN: 978-1-4809-3111-4

Memories in the Land of Stardust

Dedicated to
Linda Marie Tyndall

With great thanks and gratitude to the following: R.M. DePontes (Editor in Chief),
Sandi & Marlee Smith, Debra DePontes, Aggie, Dan & Pookie Ressel,
and Bill W...

Within the dark spaces of an unknown galaxy, light constantly twinkles. In one part of this mysterious galaxy, the beings on one particular planet gaze up at the beauty of the stars to see that suddenly the brightest flickering star is snuffed out, as if a bucket of water has doused its writhing flame. This light was a warm and familiar beacon, visible to children, their guardians, and to all other living things on this planet. For such a long time, they looked to this bright star to show them the way home during moonless nights. It was a friend to them, as familiar as any relative. Now they see that this one, special star has ceased to exist. That empty spot in the sky is like a gaping hole and all of the creatures on the planet wonder what has happened to the beautiful light. Will it return?

And then, one day, with lightning speed, and trailing dazzling sparks of color in red, blue and yellow hues, a comet streaks through the sky. Like a falling star and carrying a life that none of the creatures could have imagined, the comet strikes the Earth with thunderous force.

Since arriving on Earth in that blazing comet, and for a long, long time afterward, Star had slowly awakened. The sparkly, crystalline star child hid in the darkness that the meteor that carried him had carved into this strange planet, afraid to move. After all, what else was he to do? So far from home, so far from where his journey began, he needed to make sense of what had happened to him. His landing on this world had created a deep hole, a tunnel lined with crystals that became his sanctuary, a safe place for him to think. Until he made sense of his life, the mere thought of climbing up and out of the safety of his hole made him feel uncomfortable. The crystals lining the cave reminded Star of what little he remembered about where he was from. Beyond the mouth of the cave was nothing but the unknown. Even though he had been on this planet for quite some time, he was still much afraid.

He needed time to ponder over everything that happened in the past and what lay ahead for him. All he knew were his thoughts and his memories, broken and confusing as they were. So he continued to ponder, to struggle with recovering his shattered memory, lost in his thoughts.

Sometimes during the night, he would venture out of this crystal tunnel to explore the forest. He often sought refuge by the river as it was a secondary sanctuary for him to think about where he came from and what lay ahead. During Star's nightly walks, he met many creatures who were awake and comfortable with the darkness. In a way, Star, too, felt at ease—the darkness hid all of his differences from the creatures of a planet that, even after all of this time, was not his home.

Tonight, though, he decided to venture out during a full moonlit sky. In an attempt to slip away from the bright and revealing light, Star headed to the river. He noticed his reflection in the water, one which was so very different from all of the other beings whom Star had come to recognize from his jaunts into *their* lands. Would he ever fit in, would he ever find someone to talk to, communicate with, to share his thoughts with? Sometimes Star would hear what he thought were words directed at him from these creatures. Yet when he tried to get close to the sounds, Star would find that what he thought were words were nothing but the noises of this odd land—the slapping of water over rocks, the whistling of short bands of weeds twisting and writhing near the shore, or the cracking and swaying of huge tree branches whipped by the wind. No one was talking to him. Star knew that he might as well be listening to his own singing voice echoing off the glowing crystal walls of his empty cave. He felt so very alone.

Heading back to his crystal cave, Star recognized change was happening within the forest. Somehow, Star knew complex things about this alien world and how its creatures lived, things a child learns from those who raised him: were they parents, guides, mentors or guardians? Star could not remember who had guided him. Were they still up in the stars, the stars he has fallen from? He felt sad and alone. Even though life was different in this new world, he could remember someone, it must have been his parents, telling him important things. As he thought about what he had been taught, he tried to remember where he came from. Some memories flashed through his mind of his home somewhere among the stars, He was frustrated that he couldn't see a clear picture of his lost home. So he thought instead about change, how he had changed since landing on this strange and beautiful planet; slowly he had become braver. He loved to stand witness to the beings of this planet who like Star were undergoing changes of their own. He liked how a forest tree is taller at the end of summer than at the beginning of it; how the newborn bluebird, whose empty eggshell you found beneath its family's nest, is off and flying before you knew it. Even better, the star child loved how the fuzzy caterpillar spins a cocoon and soon enough bursts forth as a black and orange butterfly soaring in the air as its new journey begins.

Sometimes, he thought, we miss these changes. But Star knew that if we give the world a little bit of our attention, we will begin to notice life growing and changing all around us. He never forgot to look at himself, at his reflection in the river to see if he had grown an inch or if his eyes were a different sparkling shade of blue or green or purple than the week before. When he thought about his new home, the change that had most profoundly affected him, Star realized how tough and uncomfortable Earth had felt at first—and being at ease here was still not a natural feeling. After all, coming to this new home was nothing he wished or desired. Star wondered if change normally turns out well as it did for the baby bluebird and caterpillar. *Will it bring me a deeper sense of personal understanding? Will I know more about where I am and what I should do and become?* He remembered his guardians had said that change is like a ruler that will measure your experiences as long as you mark the journey of life and embrace the path that lies ahead.

Thinking about these changes tired Star out. He soon fell into a sound sleep within the safety of his tunnel-home, tucked away deep in the forest floor. Outside his snug home, many of the forest's creatures were asleep, and like Star, dreaming of the adventures that await them, not knowing what will remain the same—and what will be different—when they awake. Each of them has a different dream, some are scary visions of hidden dangers lurking in the shadows of large, rotting logs; some are happy and bright, pleasant dreams of tasty green leaves and sweet-smelling flowers covering the forest floor.

. . .

It is a warm autumn morning, and the creatures of the forest are awake. They sense a change in season for the wind is blowing hard, spinning the brightly colored red and yellow leaves around, signaling the end of summer.

The sun bursts through the white glistening rain clouds, its rays lighting up a crystal-clear blue sky and illuminating the dew on the grass blades. The mourning doves coo, as they always do, to welcome the morning on behalf of all the creatures of the forest. "It's time to get up as a new day dawns," they sing in a soft melody.

"Good morning to you, too," Annie says as she pokes her furry, feline head out from the bed of twigs and leaves that have kept her warm and safe from the long chilly night. She opens her mouth in a great yawn and rubs her green almond-shaped eyes with her big paws. The nearby robins sing, "Time to get up, it's a new day filled with new adventure."

"Oh, I am so very tired," she says in a yawn while pulling out the little twigs that have gotten caught in her long whiskers and silky, black and white fur. *It's always a struggle getting these little rascals out.* Her tail, prehensile and moving on its own like a big finger, snatches a large piece of

bark from her backside and tosses it lightly into the overgrowth. *What a pain!* She thinks.

Annie wonders: *How long have I been lost in the forest?* Somehow, she has lost all sense of time. She was so excited when she first entered the forest, exploring all the new sights and sounds, but the days have turned long and gloomy. She now misses home and all the beings she loves. Annie feels a deep loneliness when thinking about her lost loved ones. It is scary and lonely, she thinks, to be without a friend. She nibbles on some sweet-sour wild berries and rich and crunchy walnuts, thinking about her family. She misses all the comforts of a warm home and all of the scrumptious meals that she did not have to hunt, but most of all she misses the love and tenderness she received: the hugs, kisses, beautiful clothing and the way they treated her like a daughter, bringing her everywhere as they would a child of their own. Her family loved nature and enjoyed camping and on one particular trip, they decided to bring Annie along. Annie remembers climbing up a tree jumping from tree to tree, and with her "weird monkey tail" (as mama used to call it), she flew like a bird as her tail grabbed the branches of each tree. Faster and faster she moved and farther and deeper into the forest and further away from her loved ones. With a belly full of berries and walnuts, Annie settles into a restful nap.

Suddenly, Annie is awakened by a loud thump. The ground is shaking violently all around her. *Yikes!* "What was that?" Annie blurts out. With fright-filled, glistening eyes Annie looks out to see a marvelous dazzling sparkle of colors brightly radiating from a hole in front of her. *Oh my! What is this? Better get up and find out.* With trepidation, she lightly scampers over to a large hole just beside a fallen tree to take a closer look.

What she sees is beyond her comprehension or imagination, for there stands a beautiful, sapphire-eyed little creature smiling at her.

"Hello, black and white cat," the shimmering little creature says.

"Are you referring to me?" Annie's face wrinkles, puzzled.

"You understand me?" A film of moisture suddenly coats the creature's sparkling eyes. Annie thinks how happy, or rather, how relieved, he looks. "To answer your question, yes," Star says, "Your long white whiskers and pointy ears seem to resemble a cat to me."

With pride, Annie replies, "A cat perhaps, but I am a girl, and my name is Annie Fanny!" With a soft and timid voice, she asks the shimmering little creature, "Are you a boy or girl? You look so very different than anyone I have ever seen before." Her wiggly tail sways back and forth, almost as if it is wary of the unfamiliar creature.

"It's nice to meet you, Annie. I call myself Star. I am not a boy or girl; I am a child. My memory is a bit foggy. I don't know from where I came, but I feel my real home is very far from here. I have been scared and thinking a lot about what has happened to me since I arrived in your forest. I thought for so long that it has felt like how I would imagine being frozen in time would feel. I was stuck, you could say, until you came along just now." He shifts his feet as if nervous, and Annie is astounded by the glittering colors streaming through his crystalline body.

And then Star adds, "But, in some uncertain way I feel as though I have been here before. I look very different because that's how my parents made me. I am translucent, and you can see everything through me. I am connected to everything and everything is connected to me! In your world I look like an exotic opal, a gemstone that you may not be familiar with."

Oh how wonderful, Annie feels. *What a unique creature I have met. Maybe Star can be my friend?* Excitedly she asks, "Would you like to play? I can lead the way because the forest is my domain!"

"No, no, I shall lead the way, my new found friend, says Star. I will show you another way to play on this very special day together. This might be your domain, but I have found some things that you might not have seen before. We can often miss the things that are right in front of us. Look at me meeting you. Who knows how many times we missed each other while walking through this forest?" A slit of silver forms where Annie imagines his mouth to be: *He's smiling at me!* She thinks.

Annie agrees and follows Star down a long and narrow brush-filled path. After walking for a mile or two they pause for a moment to rest, and Annie softly says to Star, "My paws are getting wet and soiled from the morning dew and I was grooming them for hours before."

Shrugging and seemingly without care or worry, Star replies, "Just hop on my back. Even though I landed next to you with a thunderous crash, I can make myself as light as a helium balloon; we will float down the path together." With

a warm sense of trust, Annie hops on her new friend's back and they continue down the path, skipping and bouncing along. It is a joyous ride for both as they drift along and eventually reach the river's edge.

"Oh, no," Annie frightfully cries out. "I have never played in water before. There is nowhere for me to jump, hide, play, and lay." Tears start flowing from Annie's eyes. *I do not want to disappoint my new friend, but my heart trembles because of my fear of water. I have to be honest with him if we are to be friends.*

Star says, "I understand your fear...fear can be an excuse for not trying something new." Annie listens intently. "Trust me; I was afraid for so long I lost count of the days. My fear kept me from going very far into the forest. Yet had I not overcome my fear, I would never have met you today! Fear may feel comfortable if we never let go of it, but freedom from our fear can lead to something greater. Fear is, too often, just an excuse for hiding out, for not trying new things. We shall never know until we take the leap or at least try. I know your fear holds you back but do not fret, as you will not regret, nor will you forget, the journey we are about to take, as I come from a distant place, from a time and place I do not quite remember. So come float down the river with me to see what we can see."

With the soothing and reassuring words from Star, Annie agrees and the two of them hop on a large branch that has washed up against the bank of the river. They push themselves away from the bank and slowly float down the river together.

Oh how wonderful, Annie thinks, a large smile enveloping her face. She had always been afraid of water, but her new friend's words give her the courage to leap free from her fears. Not having her paws on the ground or her tail grasping a branch has always been scary to her, yet in this moment she is put at ease by all the beautiful sights and sounds of their gentle float down the river. *Everything looks so very different on the river,* she thinks.

Oh, what is this? She wonders, as a giant dragonfly buzzes very near to her ear and whispers, "Welcome to the river where all our dreams flow from."

That is strange, she thinks. Turning to Star with puzzlement, she asks, "Why do the stones not talk?"

Star replies, "Some things talk, some things feel, and the stones are feeling us gliding over them right now."

"Oh, what a beautiful and enchanted place the river is!" Annie says excitedly. Star replies, "This is just the beginning of our magical and colorful journey together. At least I hope so. As long as you hope so too we can make it last."

Feeling the beauty of the river, she looks down to see her reflection rippling along with the new fallen leaves flowing with rhythmic harmony. Annie closes her eyes, listening closely to the peaceful sounds that fill the air all around her.

Suddenly and without warning, calmness turns to chaos: the winds start to howl and darkness roars in, filling the once crystal-blue sky. The sky is heavy with dark clouds that unleash a fury of torrential rain, pouring down hard on the two. Annie's eyes are filled with terror as they move swiftly down the river together, being whipped harshly by the power of the gale. Faster and faster the storm drives the rising river that consumes rocks and stones, whipping against their hard edges.

Star quivers, wondering, *Is it even possible to navigate this now? No storm I have seen since my time here has ever been as powerful and strong to hit the river and forest before.* He catches his breath calling out to Annie, "Hold on—we will get through this no matter how uncertain or difficult it might seem!"

Annie's paws start to shake and her rain-drenched furry body quivers as she holds on as tight as she can. The river seizes control of their destiny.

Pounding, swishing, swaying, crashing, and smashing, the storm continues to lash out with a vicious roar! The uncontrollable forces of the river beat at Star and Annie as they fight to hang on tight to each other. Star calls out for Ms. Weedy's who he's seen before but never spoken to. He needs her help but she cannot hear him as the sounds of thunder fill the air. The lightning bursts from above, illuminating the terror in Annie's face. Annie is certain they will go under.

Then a voice shrilly shatters the air and says, "Grab on to my vines! I think I am much stronger than at any time before and I can beat this nasty storm." Annie and Star grab onto Ms. Weedy's long vines and hang on for dear life. Ms. Weedy clutches her sinewy forehead and grimaces. She is conflicted because she knows that her teeny weenie offspring need her protection as well as the rain to grow and thrive. She also knows these two innocent creatures are in serious danger. Although Ms. Weedy knows her children need her to survive the storm, she decides that she must risk some injury to her vines to save Annie

and Star. The rain continues to hammer down as the wind blows furiously all around them. Ms. Weedy cries, "I am not as strong as I thought, and I may not be able to weather this storm without more help. I will call on Oakie; he is the mightiest tree in the forest."

Ms. Weedy calls out for Oakie, the largest tree in the forest. His many branches and limbs are fully functional arms, each armored in thick chunks of dark brown bark and laced with moss. His trunk is strong, like a castle tower and far tougher than any other mighty tree could ever hope to be.

"Hello, Ms. Weedy. I was preparing to doze off to sleep," says Oakie. "How can I help you again? I know that is the reason why you call out for me."

"No, no, Oakie, this time it is not all about me. It concerns two creatures on the river," Ms. Weedy quickly replies.

Annie and Star continue to hold on tightly to Ms. Weedy as the rain pounds harder, beating them back and forth. Responding to Ms. Weedy's distressed voice, he says, "How can I help these two creatures? I don't want to get into any conflict you may have with Sid, the River King." Oakie's wooden brow furrows.

"No! No!" Ms. Weedy cries out again. "I am trying to help out two creatures that were enjoying the river until the storm roared through and now they are holding onto me. However, I am not as strong as I thought, and I will soon need to break away; otherwise all my teeny weenies will not survive—they rely on me for strength and nourishment to live."

"Well, Ms. Weedy, what can I do? I am some distance from the river." Oakie says in his loud, echoing voice.

Ms. Weedy replies, "I think your limbs are long and very strong." She bats her big, leafy eyelashes. "And I thought you might be able to pick them up and hoist them to safety."

"No need to flirt with me, Ms. Weedy. All the forest knows I am mighty and strong and I am a friend to anyone who calls this place home. Let me see how far I can stretch." He stretches and stretches until he starts to bend and then he says, "I cannot stretch anymore or I will snap and break, as I have had a trunk problem for quite a while now. Maybe, if I get rid of some of the brittle branches that are weighing me down... Humph. This makes me feel uncomfortable, I will have you know. However, I have not lived this long, grown this

strong, without reaching beyond my comfort zone from time to time." Oakie breaks off the dried up branches that have been holding him back and resumes stretching out his longest limb, but it is just too short to reach Star and Annie.

"I am sorry, Ms Weedy, I have tried, but I feel as though my trunk might just give out and the rest of the trees need me. Unfortunately, I am not of much help to your friends. Why don't you ask Sid the great River King for help?" says Oakie.

"Well," Ms. Weedy replies, "I am a bit embarrassed. I have been growing out of control and blocking some of the river that needs to flow to the forest. Sid says I have been trying to take over the river and he is the king."

Oakie replies, "I believe Sid the River King is the only one who can help your friends out. I will speak to Sid and see what I can do because everyone in the forest is a friend of mine."

Oakie calls out to the River King with all the force and strength of his leaves and they rumble and shake, until Sid the River King, in his loud and powerful voice, says, "What is the meaning of this, Oakie? It has been a long time since I heard from you; we have grown apart since you have become larger and stronger." Sid continues on, "I was trying to get comfortable for a long winter's rest when I felt a thump and a bump and the ground shook all around. And now a storm is roaring through as I was ready to take my long nap. Oh well, what else does a river do but rest?"

"It's too early to fall asleep; the fall has just begun," Oakie replies.

Sid says, "I know, but I have not felt important over the last few seasons, so I have decided to rest now and through the winter."

"Even though you felt you weren't important then, you are most certainly important now as two creatures need your help!" Oakie hastily responds.

"Hmmm," the River King says as he quietly ponders Oakie's words, wondering how he might be of help to these two creatures. They were caught in the storm while just enjoying a part of his creation, after all. *Perhaps I could open up a stream for them to ride on…or maybe two or three, or even more, something that could whisk them out of trouble?* Excited with the sudden belief that he might just be able to save two creatures from this brutal storm, he realizes that doing them a favor might lead to his own salvation. He would never tell Oakie or these creatures, or especially the beautiful Ms. Weedy, but dark feelings that he has become insignificant and without purpose have penetrated the cracks in his deep, clay riverbed and some days he has felt sad and lonely. Now, though, he suddenly feels useful.

The River King, just to clarify the situation, asks Oakie, "How did you find out about this problem? I should have known first as you are too far away."

"Well, Ms. Weedy called on me for help, thinking I could reach and pull them to safety, but my limbs are not long enough."

"Why didn't Ms. Weedy call on me, as I am the closest and the only one who can help?" The River King voice pours out with a great rumbling sound.

"Ms. Weedy thought that you were perturbed with her and her weedy family because they took over the river the last several years by growing out of control," Oakie replies.

"It's okay. I have long forgotten about such things like that. I just thought Ms. Weedy didn't need me anymore. She hardly ever talks to me."

Oakie calls out to Ms. Weedy, "The River King has forgiven you."

"Oh, thank you so much! I knew you would come around, great River King!" Ms. Weedy says while batting her leafy green eyelashes again.

Annie and Star continue to hold tightly to Miss Weedy, terrified of the storm.

Ms. Weedy starts to feel the stress on her brittle vines; the thought of her teeny weenie family's need for her strength gives her the will to let Annie and Star hold on to her for just a tad longer. Star says, "O' great River King, we desperately need your help or we shall not survive this storm."

Annie quickly chimes in, "Yes, great River King! We need you to help us out of this terrible storm." Her little voice quivers as she is wet and cold and chilled to the bone. The River King looks at Star and realizes he has seen a shimmering glow like this one before, a sparkling array of colors just like those coming from this being's skin. Not long ago a shimmering comet blazed across the sky and shook the earth when it hit the ground. He asks, "Are you not the one who caused a thump and a bump and then the ground shook around, creating many cracks in the ground?"

"Yes, River King. I am the one; however, I did not intentionally land in the middle of the forest. I had no control over the journey that brought me to the forest. I am so sorry if it has caused the forest and all its creature great distress."

Sid, the River King, listening and understanding, is no longer so upset, and thinks he might be able to help them out of this awful mess. *I shall make use of these cracks and crevices and bring the two of them to safety.*

Suddenly, with a huge gush, the River King forces the river into new channels. Star and Annie feel the urgent pull of the waters and know it is time to let go of Ms. Weedy. Expressing their profound thanks, they quickly say goodbye, feeling the forces of the river's undercurrent just below the surface water, pulling them in a new direction. Up and down, Annie and Star go bobbing and bouncing along and then, right in front of their eyes, the river divides itself into many streams that branch out through the forest. Those streams eagerly seek the empty ravines and areas in the forest that are dry and thirsty. The River King grows calmer as he spreads himself into many channels and over hundreds of miles, moving deeper into the forest. The River King is now spread far beyond Annie and Star who ride the foaming bubbles, feeling they will soon be safe.

All over the forest, ponds and lakes spring up. The creatures of the forest flock to the birth of these new waterways rushing in all directions, bringing life to areas that were dying. The creatures feel the heart of the forest beating and see the veins of the forest flowing with lush waters.

Annie and Star feel the water slow down greatly as the rains subside. They scramble to the riverbank as the clouds part and the sun beams down on all of them. Sid catches his breath, looking with awe at a huge river roaring past him where moments before there was only dry and dying forest. He mumbles, "Oh wow, that was quite a wild one, I must say."

Slowly, water from the river begins to pool around Annie and Star and they both witness a new pond being formed. Birds, rabbits, frogs and many hundreds of animals, insects and less familiar creatures begin to sing. Their strange voices grow louder and join together; like a wild symphony they all sing joyfully, praising the birth of new waterways within the forest.

Annie and Star hug each other, looking deeply into one another's eyes. They recognize for the first time the unique spirit within the other. They see happiness in the other, and they know that their rough journey down the river together has been worth the moments of fear. Annie sees a reflection of herself in Star, and Star sees a reflection of himself in Annie. They both know at once and understand: *A journey in life is always filled with constant change. When I respect my surroundings, think through my actions, and have faith in others, I can be unafraid of change.*

Annie and Star stare at one another, their eyes softening with the understanding that as friends they have shared terrible danger together and survived. They look at Sid the River King and realize how instrumental he has been in bringing them to safety. "Thank you, great king," they say in unison.

The River King exclaims, "No, it is not about me; it is about the two of you and all the forest that has truly saved my life! I was becoming stale and stagnant and without change I cannot lead the way as a river king must do. There is room for all of life and only with change can it be possible. Nothing can ever remain the same; if we wish to live, we must grow."

Ms. Weedy hears this and realizes she must change, too. Her family is important, but some of her children are old enough to venture farther away and perhaps keeping them all near her, not letting them go on their own journeys, has contributed to the River King's problem. Miss Weedy had heard Sid calling out to her many times, and she had ignored him. She pretended not to need him; maybe because deep down she did not want to face the truth that she was holding on too tightly to her children, not letting them find their own adventures, and blocking the river.

Voices fill the air calling out, "Annie! Annie! Please come home, we miss you! Can you hear us?" The voices continue to call out from a place that seems so faint and far away, yet somehow close, like whispers in her mind.

Annie feels torn and conflicted. Should she go home or stay with her new-found friends. Tears flow from Annie's eyes, droplets clinging to her whiskers. But she feels in her heart she must go home to her loved ones. It took until now for her to realize how important the journey back home will be.

Annie hugs Star with gratitude for all that has been given to her and for their shared experiences and time together.

With a heavy heart, Annie says, "Goodbye, Star. I must go home now to those who love me."

Star replies, "Do not say goodbye...it hurts too much—I have lost the people I loved and have been alone on this strange world for so long. Yet I believe we shall soon be together again. Let us both believe that and together we can make it true."

Annie's ears flatten in sincerity as she says, "Let's make it true, then. Together. Someday I shall return to you and the forest, as you both are now a part of me."

Annie heads down the narrow path where her journey had begun and where she now realizes the voices of her loved ones are coming from. She turns around to look back to see Star smiling at her.

Star says, "Our meeting was beautiful, our journey also beautiful. I believe this beauty is just beginning to blossom." Annie hesitates. She cannot leave Star behind, and with a flick of her tail she waves him toward her, saying, "Come with me, Star."

Then together they head down the path to see what they can see. Star whispers, "I think this is the beginning of a beautiful friendship, don't you?"